As for the Princess?

A folktale from
Quebec

adapted & illustrated by

Stéphane Jorisch

Annick Press Ltd.
Toronto • New York • Vancouver

© 2001 Stéphane Jorisch (adapted text and illustrations)
Cover and text design by Sheryl Shapiro

Annick Press Ltd.

We acknowledge the support of the Canada Council for the Arts, the Ontario Arts Council, and the Government of Canada through the Book Publishing Industry Development Program (BPIDP) for our publishing activities.

Cataloging in Publication Data

Jorisch, Stéphane
  As for the princess?

ISBN 1-55037-695-0 (bound) ISBN 1-55037-694-2 (pbk.)

I. Title.

PS8569.O754A88 2001   jC843'.54   C2001-930090-5
PZ7.J67As 2001

The art in this book was rendered in water color, gouache, pen and ink and some digital work .
The text was typeset in Bernhard Modern.

Distributed in Canada by:
Firefly Books Ltd.
3680 Victoria Park Avenue
Willowdale, ON
M2H 3K1

Published in the U.S.A. by Annick Press (U.S.) Ltd.
Distributed in the U.S.A. by:
Firefly Books (U.S.) Inc.
P.O. Box 1338
Ellicott Station
Buffalo, NY 14205

Printed in Canada by Litho Mille-îles

visit us at: www.annickpress.com

Thanks Anne M. and Serge T.
S.J.

Rembrandt

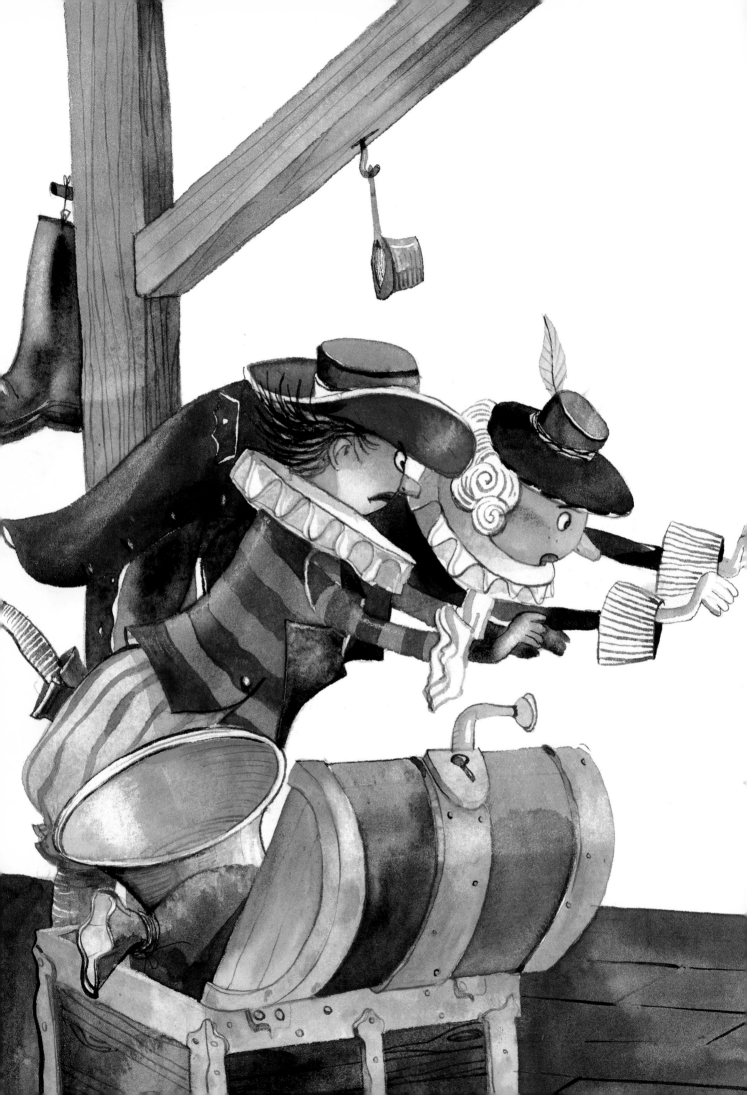

Once upon a time, in a faraway kingdom, a father left his three sons very unusual legacies. The oldest received a sack with 100,000 gold pieces, the second a horn that could summon 100,000 soldiers in a jiffy, and the youngest, a boy named Simon, an old leather belt. Proudly, Simon put the belt around his waist. Then he stretched and said, "Soon I will be all grown up. I would really like to see the beautiful Princess in the castle over the mountains."

"Oh no, you don't!" said the second brother. "She's beautiful, mean, and greedy." Too late, there was a whoosh in the air and Simon was standing in fine chambers full of silk and shiny objects, looking straight at the beautiful Princess, who had a huge frown on her face.

"Where did YOU come from?" she
wanted to know, looking him up and down.
"It had better be a good story, or else—"

"Oh, but it is," stammered Simon. "I didn't come to scare you, I just put on my father's belt and thought I would like to see YOU, the famous, beautiful—"

"Let me have a look at that belt," said the Princess, and then, without another word, she walked away with it. As for Simon, he was chased from the castle with a kick in the pants by the guards. It took him three whole days to walk back home, tired and hungry.

"Simon, Simon, Simon," said his oldest brother, when hearing the story, "the Princess is a baaaaad apple! Here, take this sack and ask her what she wants in exchange for your belt. But don't tell her how much gold you have, or she will want it all." Simon promised, and thanked his brother.

The next day he started all the way back to the
castle, carrying the heavy sack.

The beautiful Princess spotted him a mile away. She came down to her gardens and asked Simon what he wanted.

"I, um, I came to offer you this sack full of gold pieces in exchange for my belt," said Simon.

"Don't be silly," said the Princess, "you don't have that kind of fortune! Let me have a look at that."

Then, when she saw all the gold, she handed the sack to a footman and said, "I'll think about it." And Simon was chased away again with a kick in the pants. Simon's burden was light now, but his heart was heavy. It took him six days to get all the way home, tired and hungry.

"You must be joking," shouted his second brother when Simon told his story.

"She's smarter than I am," said Simon, hanging his head.

"No, she's not. She's a baaaad apple," said the brother. "You just have to keep your wits about you. If I send my 100,000 soldiers along to protect you, you must promise me to be tough. And don't come back without your belt and all the gold!"

Simon promised. He took the horn, and soon he and the entire army of 100,000 soldiers were on their way to confront the mean but beautiful Princess.

She was looking out over the south fortifications when she noticed her kingdom crawling with soldiers. Then she spotted Simon. He looked the same as the last two times, except that he had a horn slung over his shoulder and wore a tough expression.

Well, you know what happened next.

"Let me have a look at that horn," said the Princess, and before Simon could say "Noooo!" she had blown into it and the entire army had disappeared.

"Gimme back my horn," cried Simon, but the Princess said she would think about it, and walked away.

Now poor Simon was so disappointed with himself, he ran from the castle and didn't stop until he came to a strange orchard.

"Dear father," Simon cried out loud, "I have not used your gift well, and I really failed my good brothers. How am I ever going to make it up to them?"

Just then he noticed a tree full of beautiful, shiny apples. Famished, he picked three and began eating. When he was finished, he thought something strange had happened to his nose. Yes, it was definitely longer and fatter.

He wasn't pleased.

He was stumbling about and feeling his face when he saw a tree with ripe blue plums. So he picked three and ate them.

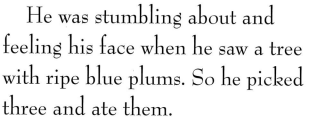

At first his nose got in the way, but as he chewed, it seemed like his nose was shrinking, and after the third plum it was back to normal.

And then Simon had such
a brilliant, naughty idea, he
almost scared himself.

Three hours later he appeared once
more at the castle. The beautiful Princess
was looking out the window and called,
"What are those shiny things in your
basket? Let me have a look at them." And
she came, picked up three apples, and
walked away with them.

Now Simon put on a
disguise and waited close
to the gates. Three
hours passed. The
Princess could be seen at a
window with a veil covering
her head. Next a carriage arrived
bearing the royal doctor in black robes, carrying a large bag. But just three
minutes later he returned to his carriage, rubbing his backside.

"The Princess is very sick," whispered the maids and the footmen and
the guards, not looking too sad about it, though.

So Simon stepped forward and announced, "I'm a traveling man
of medicine. I heal the sick with exotic herbs and roots.
Let me have a look at that Princess."

When she heard about the stranger, the Princess immediately ordered him up to her chambers. And Simon saw a very large, long nose. He took off his cape.

"What have you done?" wailed the Princess. "Look at my nose!"

"I might be able to help a little with this calamity," said Simon, "but first you have to return my brother's horn."

The Princess gave it to him in exchange for a plum from the basket. She ate it and her nose shrank a little.

"That's not good enough," she cried, and Simon asked for his other brother's sack of gold.

She handed it over in exchange for a second plum. Her nose grew smaller, but not small enough.

"I still look ugly!" she shouted.

"Well, give me back my belt," said Simon, and he put it on, just in case. Then he looked in his basket: More apples, but no more plums. "They are all gone," he said.

Furious, the Princess called for her guards. But Simon touched his belt and was whisked back home in three seconds.

He and his loyal brothers lived not forever,
but for a long and happy time.
As for the Princess? Weeell ...